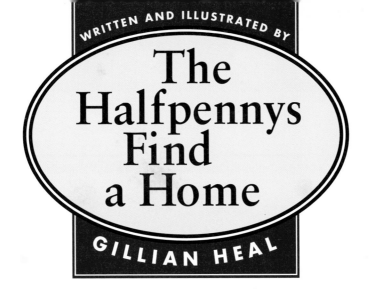

WRITTEN AND ILLUSTRATED BY

The Halfpennys Find a Home

GILLIAN HEAL

BEYOND WORDS PUBLISHING, INC.

PUBLISHED BY
Beyond Words Publishing, Inc.
13950 NW Pumpkin Ridge Road
Hillsboro, OR 97124
(503) 693-8700

TEXT AND ILLUSTRATIONS
copyright © 1994 by Gillian Heal

DESIGN
Principia Graphica

EDITORIAL
Julie Livingston

Printed in the United States
Distributed by Publishers Group West

ISBN 1-885223-04-8

For Barbara Kane

*And remembering
"Lily" and "Rosamund"*

Not long ago,
the Halfpenny family—
Ben, Laura, Mommy, Daddy, and
their spotted dog, Buttons—
lived in a small apartment.

As the children grew **bigger**,
the apartment seemed to grow smaller.

The sofa was not long enough for everyone,
the table was not big enough
for everyone to work at,
and the tiny balcony was stuffed
like a jungle with flowerpots and plants.

Even Buttons thought
his own dog house would be nice.

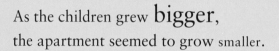

The children had shared a bedroom
since they were babies,
and Laura wished for a room of her own
where she could have her desk and her books
and could dream quietly.

Ben wanted his own space for his train,
his dinosaur, and his collections.
He wanted posters of planets and mountains
on the red walls.

They all wanted a garden.

Mommy wanted to grow vegetables.
Daddy wanted to grow roses and apple trees.
Ben thought a treehouse would be good,
and Laura wanted to write a book
in a shady arbor.

One very wet day,
they decided that finding a house
with a good roof was important.
        "And lots of windows to let in sunshine," said Laura.
"And a big kitchen with a big table so we can all cook and
paint and do homework."
        "And make models," said Ben.
        "And make a mess," said Mommy quietly.

· · · · ·

So the Halfpennys went looking for a house.
The spotted dog, Buttons, went too.
They found grumpy-looking houses with no gardens.
They found houses that were too small or too big.

They found houses that were already SOLD
and houses that belonged to other families. Ben and Laura held
their mother's hands and wondered if they would ever find
a house for their family—anywhere.

And then they turned a corner. . . .

and there was a house that was just
the right size, and it had lots of windows.
There was a big notice on the picket fence
that said FOR SALE.
"Oh! Oh!" cried Laura.
"It's so pretty!"

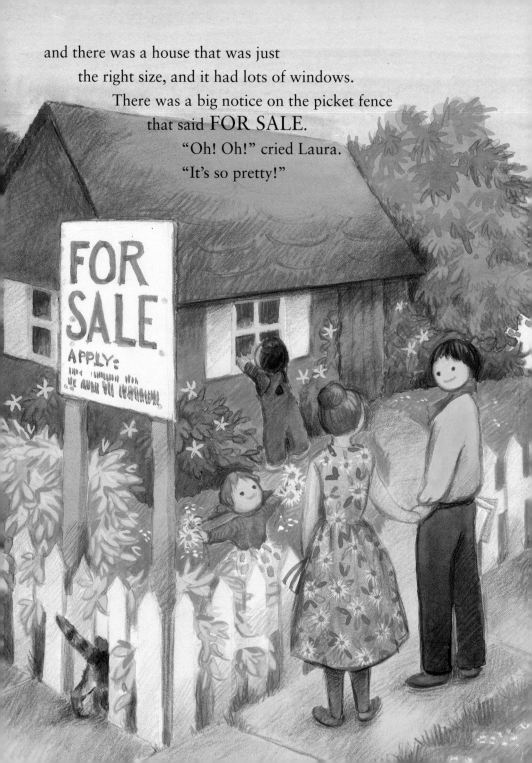

"That looks like the house for us,"
said Daddy.
    And Buttons thought so too.
    His doghouse would fit neatly 'round the side,
    under a tree in the garden.

Mommy and Daddy went to the bank
to arrange to buy the house.

Then Mommy went shopping with Ben
to buy a big new table.

Ben looked at everything in the apartment.
    "How are we going to get ALL THIS STUFF
to the new house?" he asked.
    "We are going to pack it all into boxes," said Daddy.
"We must be careful not to lose the little things,
and the fragile things must be wrapped up in paper
so they won't get broken.
You can help."

"Dinosaurs don't get packed in boxes!"

said Ben decidedly,
and he stuffed Dinosaur
into his backpack
with his head sticking out
so he could see.

Laura struggled with a heavy book,
and Ben got lost behind a picture.
It had not seemed nearly so big hanging on the wall.
The children were very busy.

Saucepans with handles,
coffeepots with long spouts,
and the fat, round cookie jar
were hard to pack.
"Life is full of such awkward shapes!"
cried Mommy.

"Look what I found,"
said Laura, holding up a frying pan
with a long, long handle.
Together, she and Mommy worked out
how to pack it in a box.

When all the packing was done, Ben realized
that the apartment which had always been his home
was empty. Home wasn't there any more.
He gave the dinosaur an encouraging hug
and said, "Don't cry, Dinosaur.
We are going to our new house."

Then friends came to help move the furniture
and carry the heaviest boxes. At last, everything
was loaded into the truck.
At the new house, Ben and Laura helped
carry things inside.
It was exciting making
a new home.

The big new table

KITCHEN

Everything was taken out of the truck: chairs and pillows,
beds and bedding, rugs, curtains, the dog's old dish,
precious plants, Grandma's painting of Grandpa,
all of Mommy's hats, Daddy's big black boots,
little red and yellow boots, everybody's clothes,
and boxes and boxes of stuff.

rrived from the store.

That night Ben and Laura slept in their own rooms for the first time.

Ben felt very little all alone in the new place,
but then Mommy and Daddy came to tuck him in and say
"Sweet dreams."
"Sweet dreams, Dinosaur too," he said,
and he snuggled down in his old familiar bed

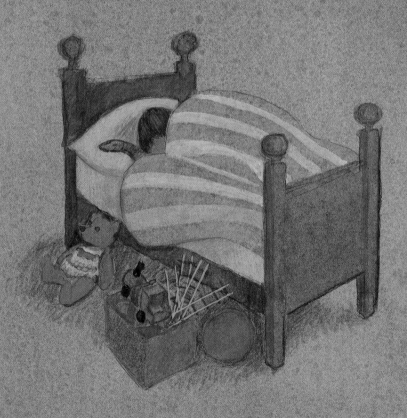

and was soon fast asleep.

Mommy and Daddy were tired too.

They fell asleep in the middle
of their heaped-up house. . .
and so did Buttons.

Eventually all the boxes were empty
and everything was in place.
The new paint dried and
the windows sparkled.
Friends came over for supper
to celebrate.

· · · · ·

The Halfpennys now live in their new house
happily and crossly, noisily and quietly.
They laugh and cry and hug.
They have a place to be a family.

And a little stripy cat
has found a new home too.